red

NEAL PORTER BOOKS

HOLIDAY HOUSE / NEW YORK

dark red

light red

lost red

bright red

rose red

# mud red

rust red

# blood red

apple red

brick red

autumn red

trick red

caged red

rage red

trust red

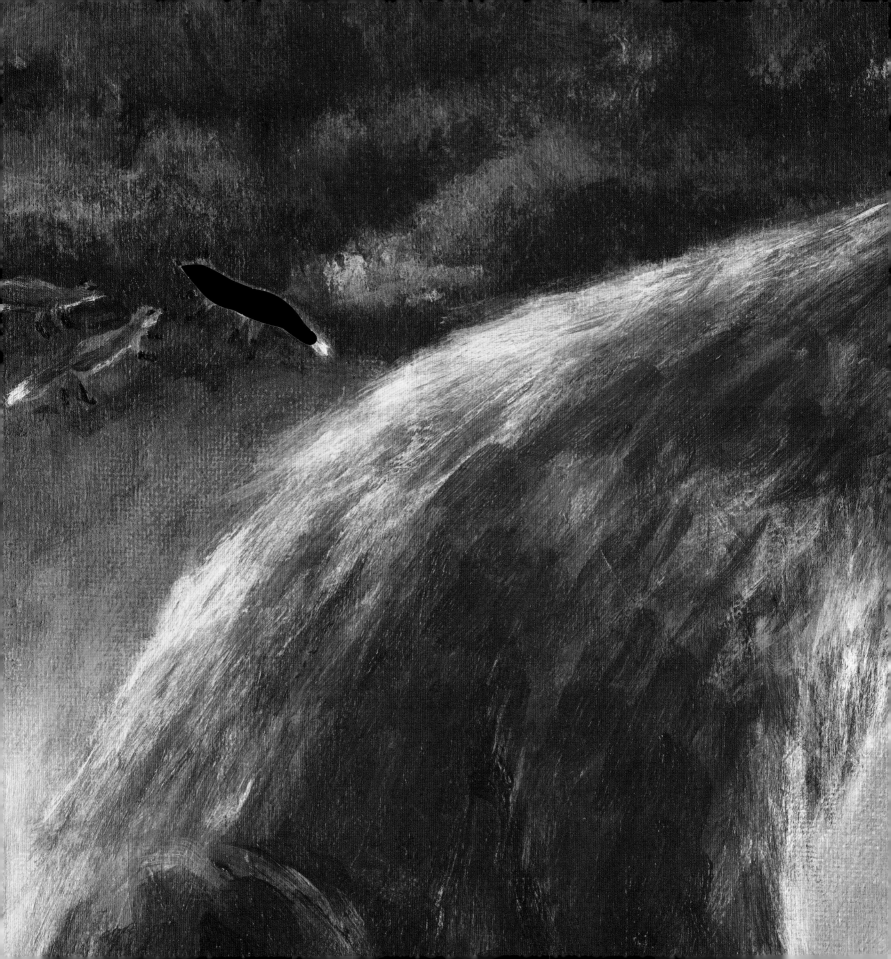

just red

## About *Red*

I've always been fascinated by the ways in which color can evoke emotion.

In 2007, I began working on a book with an environmental theme using color as a focal point. That came to fruition in *Green*, published in 2012. *Green* was always meant to stand alone, but sometimes a book tells an author that it needs to be written, and that's what happened with *Blue*, rooted in loyalty and loss, and published in 2018.

Around that time, after expressing my concern about the great divisiveness that had taken hold in our world, my dear friend and longtime editor Neal Porter encouraged me to channel those feelings into a book. And so, *Red* was conceived. Red as in anger and discord, but also as in love and compassion.

I believe that readers should be left to make their own connections with characters in books, but in my mind, the boy who we watch grow up in *Blue* is the father of the little girl we see at the end of *Green*. And a few years later, that little girl plays a pivotal role in *Red*.

—Laura Vaccaro Seeger

## For Neal

Neal Porter Books

Text and illustrations copyright © 2021 by Laura Vaccaro Seeger
All Rights Reserved
HOLIDAY HOUSE is registered in the U.S. Patent and Trademark Office.
Printed and bound in June 2021 at Leo Paper, Heshan, China.
The artwork for this book was created using acrylic paint on canvas.
www.holidayhouse.com
First Edition
1  3  5  7  9  10  8  6  4  2

Library of Congress Cataloging-in-Publication Data

Names: Seeger, Laura Vaccaro, author.
Title: Red / by Laura Vaccaro Seeger.
Description: First edition. | New York : Holiday House, [2021] | "A Neal
Porter Book." | Audience: Ages 4 to 8. | Audience: Grades K–1. |
Summary: Illustrations and simple, rhyming text follow a young fox as it
searches for a way home, through a world of many shades of red, after
being separated from its family.
Identifiers: LCCN 2020044134 | ISBN 9780823447121 (hardcover)
Subjects: CYAC: Stories in rhyme. | Foxes—Fiction. | Red—Fiction.
Classification: LCC PZ8.3.S4504 Red 2021 | DDC [E]—dc23
LC record available at https://lccn.loc.gov/2020044134

ISBN 978-0-8234-4712-1 (hardcover)